CREEPY RIDDLES

Katy Hall and Lisa Eisenberg
pictures by S. D. Schindler

Dial Books for Young Readers
New York

Published by Dial Books for Young Readers
A member of Penguin Putnam Inc.
375 Hudson Street
New York, New York 10014

The Dial Easy-to-Read logo is a registered trademark of
Dial Books for Young Readers,
a member of Penguin Putnam Inc.
®TM 1,162,718.
First Edition
5 7 9 10 8 6 4

Library of Congress
Cataloging in Publication Data
Hall, Katy.
Creepy riddles/by Katy Hall and Lisa Eisenberg;
pictures by S. D. Schindler.
p.   cm.
ISBN 0-8037-1684-2 (tr.)—ISBN 0-8037-1685-0 (lib.)
1. Riddles. 2. Supernatural—Juvenile humor.
[1. Riddles. 2. Supernatural—Wit and humor.] I. Eisenberg, Lisa.
II. Schindler, S. D., ill. III. Title.
PN6371.5.H375   1998   818'.5402—DC20
94-37524   CIP   AC   r94

The full-color artwork was prepared using pen-and-ink
and watercolor washes.

Reading Level 2.1

To Lisa Eisenberg
K.H.
To Katy Hall
L.E.

To Julia—still
a riddle, but not a
creepy one!
S.D.S.

What do werewolves
say when they meet?

"Howl do you do?"

What do you call
a room full of ghosts?

A bunch of boo-boos!

How do skeletons
send their mail?

By Bony Express.

What do witches like to eat
for dessert?

Ice scream!

Why does Dracula buy the newspaper every night?

So he can read his horror-scope.

Why do witches
wear green eye shadow?

They like the way
it matches their teeth.

What moves through the air,
casts spells, and has no name?

An unidentified flying sorcerer.

How did
the monster football team
win the game?

They kicked a field ghoul!

What would you get
if you crossed a skeleton
and a jar of peanut butter?

Bones that stick to the
roof of your mouth!

What kind of stories
do little ghosts tell
around the campfire?

People stories.

How did the werewolf
send his valentines?

By hairmail!

Which witches like to play croquet?

Wicket witches!

How does a witch
with a broken broom
get to the second floor?

She takes the scarecase.

Why did the little fiends
join the protest march?

They thought it was a *demon*stration.

Why didn't the little skeleton
want to go to the party?

Because he had no
body to dance with!

What magic words
does a scary godmother
use to do her laundry?

"Wishy-washy!"

What do ghosts love to eat
for dinner?

Ghoulash.

Why is Frankenstein
so helpful?

He's always willing
to give you a hand!

Why did Granny Monster
knit her grandson three socks?

Because she heard
he'd grown another foot.

Where do demons go at night?

Out with their ghoulfriends!

What do sea monsters
like to eat?

Fish-and-ships!

What did the little ghost
order at the restaurant?

Spookghetti!

What do zombies like to drink?

*Croak*a-Cola!

Why are witch twins
so confusing?

You can never tell
which witch is which!

Why did the Frankenstein
monster get a tummy ache?

He kept *bolting* his food!

What color is a chilly ghost?

Boo!

What trees do zombies
like best?

Ceme-trees!

What do ghouls like to do
at the amusement park?

Ride the roller ghoster!

What do vampires eat at baseball games?

Fangfurters!

Why is the mad scientist
never lonely?

He's good at *making*
new friends!

Why did everyone call
the vampire crazy?

They heard he'd gone batty!

What do ghosts put on their mashed potatoes?

Grave-y!

What did the zombie eat
after he had a tooth taken out?

The dentist!

What fairy tale is scary enough
to tell little witches?

Ghouldilocks and the Three Scares.

Why did Frankenstein
fall in love with the witch?

She *swept* him off his feet!

Why did the little witch
get a prize in school?

She was the best
*spell*er in her class.

What kind of milk do you get
from a ghost cow?

Evaporated milk!

What do ghosts
wear when it's raining?

*Boot*s.

What game do little zombies play at birthday parties?

Swallow the leader!

What do you get if you cross
a giant with a vampire?

A *big* pain in the neck!

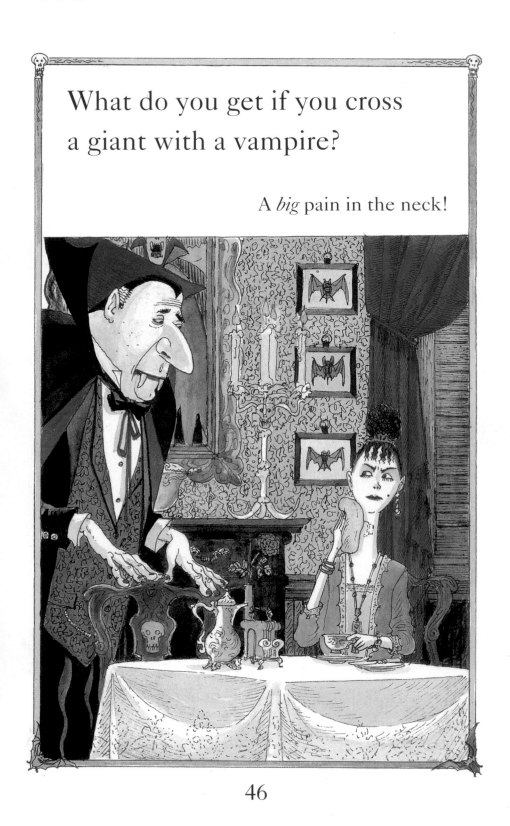

What did the little vampire say to the judges when he won the Batboy Contest?

"Fangs a lot!"

What did the ghost bride
throw to her bridesmaids?

Her *boo*quet!